A Midsummer Night's Fairytale

Adapted by Suzanne Tye

"To my husband for all his love and support."
Suzanne.

CAST LIST

KING ARTHUR – King of Fairyland
LADY GUINEVERE – betrothed to King Arthur
WICKED STEPMOTHER– Red Riding Hood's step mother
RED RIDING HOOD – Stepdaughter of Wicked Stepmother
HANSEL – in love with Red Riding Hood
BIG BAD WOLF– wants to eat Red Riding Hood
GOLDILOCKS – wants the Wolf's fur for a new coat
CAPTAIN OF THE GUARD
COURTIER
Court JESTER – Master of Entertainment
CANDY KING – King of Candy land
QUEEN OF HEARTS – Married to Candy King
PETER - Works for Candy King
PAN – Works for Candy King
ACE OF HEARTS – Courtier of the Queen of Hearts
ACE OF SPADES– Courtier of the Queen of Hearts
ACE OF DIAMONDS– Courtier of the Queen of Hearts
ACE OF CLUBS– Courtier of the Queen of Hearts
CARD 1 - Servant of the Queen of Hearts
CARD 2 - Servant of the Queen of Hearts
CARD 3 - Servant of the Queen of Hearts
CARD 4 - Servant of the Queen of Hearts
BLIND MICE 1 - plays Prologue
BLIND MICE 2 - plays Prologue
BLIND MICE 3 - plays Prologue
PUSS 'N BOOTS – plays Prince Charming
TROLL – plays Cinderella
PRINCE CHARMING – plays Ball
STRAW MAN – plays the Pumpkin
RAPUNZEL – plays the Clock
FIRST BEAR - actor in MacBear
SECOND BEAR - actor in MacBear
THIRD BEAR - actor in MacBear
FIRST HAM - actor in Ham-Let
SECOND HAM - actor in Ham-Let
THIRD HAM - actor in Ham-Let
GRETEL - actor in Hansel and Gretel

SCENE 1 - KING ARTHUR'S COURT

Enter KING ARTHUR & GUINEVERE with JESTER, COURTIER, CAPTAIN and attendants.

KING ARTHUR
> Now, fair Guinevere, our nuptial hour
> Draws on apace, four happy days bring in
> Another moon – but O, methinks, how slow
> This old moon wanes…

GUINEVERE (interrupts in a panic)
> Four days! But there so much to do! We need a cake, decorations, invitations (she gasps) And the entertainment! What about the entertainment Arthur?

KING ARTHUR
> Jester!

JESTER comes forward with an elaborate bow.

> What entertainment is prepared for our wedding day, to stir up our guests to mirth and merriment?

JESTER
> A play, sire, performed by the Royal Jester Theatre Company?

GUINEVERE
> Oh Arthur, I love a good play - a romantic one that makes you laugh.

KING ARTHER
> Yes, something with a bit of action and a fight. We will have the greatest play ever performed in all of Fairyland!

JESTER bows again

> Go. Tell the people that anyone may submit their play and the best will be chosen for the wedding feast.

JESTER

> Anyone your highness… Even amateurs? *(He looks disgusted)*

KING ARTHUR

> Yes, anyone. Now go.

Exit JESTER.

KING ARTHUR

> Captain of the Guard.

CAPTAIN steps forward & salutes.

KING ARTHUR

> Is everything prepared for our hunt?

CAPTAIN

> Yes, my Lord, we will be leaving for the woods at dawn's first light.

KING ARTHUR

> Excellent.

CAPTAIN

> We should be back in plenty of time for the wedding.

GUINEVERE

> You're going hunting before the wedding?

KING ARTHUR

> Of Course! *(GUINEVERE looks upset)* Guinevere do not fret my love, we will wed with pomp, with triumph and with revelling.

COURTIER

> Presenting Wicked Stepmother, and her step daughter Red Riding Hood, Hansel and the Big Bad Wolf.

*Enter WICKED STEPMOTHER, BIG BAD WOLF, HANSEL, RED
RIDING HOOD, as their names are announced. The WICKED
STEPMOTHER rushes forward and bows low to KING ARTHUR.*

WICKED STEPMOTHER
>King Arthur, oh renowned ruler!

KING ARTHUR
>Greetings, good Wicked Stepmother. What's the news
>with you?

WICKED STEPMOTHER
>Full of vexation come I, with a complaint against my step
>daughter little Red Riding Hood.
>
>Come, Big Bad Wolf. *(She pushes the BIG BAD WOLF
>forward)*
>
>My noble lord, I would give my step daughter in marriage
>to this fine wolf. But Hansel, the German exchange
>student, has wooed her with pretzels, gingerbread men
>and candy canes. *(She points at HANSEL)* You with your
>lederhosen and umpapa boy band good looks.
>
>Now she refuses to marry the Big Bad Wolf. She is
>disobedient!   And as her wicked step mother, I will
>dispose of her! *(Realizes her mistake)* Eh… may dispose
>of her either in marriage to this wolf or to be locked in a
>tower for a hundred years, according to the laws of
>Fairyland.

KING ARTHUR
>What say you little Red Riding Hood?

RED RIDING HOOD kneels before him.

RED RIDING HOOD
>Your Majesty, just last week my Wicked Stepmother sent
>me into the woods to visit my grandmother. Little did I
>know she had devised an evil plan. She had sent the Big

Bad Wolf ahead to grandma's, where he waited to gobble
me up! If it had not been for the woodcutter, I would not
be here today. Now she would have me marry the wolf
knowing that if I refuse I will be locked in a tower.

KING ARTHUR

These are the laws of our land. How else would we
maintain a steady supply of maidens in towers? You have
four days to decide your fate. Marry this fine
young...er... Wolf or be locked in a tower.

BIG BAD WOLF

Relent, my sweet little Red Riding Hood, and Hansel -
yield! She is mine by right.

HANSEL

Never!

WICKED STEPMOTHER

You're not in Germany any more Hansel.

HANSEL

Bevare volf! For I vould have you know that you did
recently catch the eye of the voodcutter's daughter,
Goldilocks, who now pursues you.

KING ARTHUR

I must confess that I have heard so much. Goldilocks
desires your hide for a new fur coat. But with the wedding
I have not given it much thought. Come, Wicked Step
Mother and Big Bad Wolf let us continue in private.
Come Guinevere. *(to RED RIDING HOOD)* You have
four days to decide.

Exit all except HANSEL and RED RIDING HOOD.

HANSEL

How now my love? Vhy, your rosy red cheeks have gone
so pale.

RED RIDING HOOD
> I think I am going to cry.

HANSEL
> Ya, me too. (Sighs) Zhe course of true love never did run smooth.

RED RIDING HOOD bursts into tears.

> Vait! Listen to me little Red Riding Hood, ve could run avay! I know of a little place deep vithin the voods. A cute cottage made of candy and sveets, vhere ve could hide. No vun vould ever find us.

RED RIDING HOOD *(Wiping away her tears)*
> Run? Through the woods? Why that sounds like a delightful idea, Hansel.

HANSEL
> Wunderbar! Look here comes Goldilocks.

Enter GOLDILOCKS, looking grumpy.

RED RIDING HOOD
> Fair Goldilocks, where are you going?

GOLDILOCKS
> Fair! Why do you mock me? Nothing is fair. I've seen the way Big Bad Wolf looks at you. Wide eyes, tongue hanging out, teeth gleaming. Oh, for I would have his fur for a new winter coat. Yet it is you he wants.

RED RIDING HOOD
> I run from him, yet he pursues me.

GOLDILOCKS
> I chase him and he flees from me.

RED RIDING HOOD
>The more I hate, the more he follows me.

GOLDILOCKS
>The more I chase, the more he hates me.

RED RIDING HOOD
>Take comfort; he no more shall see my face;
>For Hansel and myself will fly this place.

HANSEL
>Ya, tomorrow night Red Riding Hood and I vill run avay
>into the voods. Zhe Big Bad Volf vill be all yours.

RED RIDING HOOD *(earnestly)*
>Until the morning, my truest love.

HANSEL *(romantically)*
>I'll count zhe hours, my dearest dove.

GOLDILOCKS looks disgusted. Exit RED RIDING HOOD.

HANSEL
>Auf weidersehen, Goldilocks.

Exit HANSEL.

GOLDILOCKS (to the audience)
>I will go tell the wolf of Riding Hood's flight,
>Then to the wood will he tomorrow night,
>Purse them.
>And I will be right behind him.

Exit GOLDILOCKS.

SCENE 2 - THE TOWN

Enter JESTER and COURTIER. To the audience.

COURTIER
>   Hear ye, hear ye, all fairy tale characters! Hear this
>   message from your King.

JESTER
>   His Royal Highness, King Arthur, declares that all the
>   world's a stage, and all men and women merely players,
>   therefore he calls any man or woman that wishes - to
>   prepare a play for his wedding day. The play that is
>   preferred in all Fairyland will be performed before the
>   King and his new Queen at their wedding feast.

All Exit.

SCENE 3 - *THE TOWN*

*Enter STRAW MAN, PUSS 'N BOOTS, TROLL, PRINCE
CHARMING & RAPUNZEL followed shortly after by the 3 BLIND
MICE.*

BLIND MICE 1
>   Is all our company here?

BLIND MICE 2
>   Puss 'n Boots!

BLIND MICE 3
>   Prince charming!

BLIND MICE 1
>   Troll!

BLIND MICE 2
>   Rapunzel!

BLIND MICE 3
Straw man!

TROLL
What's happening?

STRAWMAN
The play, remember?

PRINCE CHARMING
We are ready, my dear friends.

BLIND MICE 2
King Arthur has requested a play be performed on his
wedding feast. A play of romance, of fighting, and of
humour. Therefore, we the 3 Blind Mice Theatre
Company, have found such a play, and you shall play the
parts.

BLIND MICE 3
Here is the list of every character's name, which is
thought fit, throughout fairyland, to play a part in the
performance before the king on his wedding day at night.

PUSS 'N BOOTS
First, Blind Mice, tell us what the play is about and then
read out the parts and so grow to a point.

BLIND MICE 3
Right, our play is the most lamentable romance and cruel
death of Prince Charming and Cinderella.

PUSS 'N BOOTS
Oh, a classic! A very good piece of work, I assure you.
Now, Blind Mice, read the list of parts. Masters, spread
yourselves.

They spread themselves into a line.

BLIND MICE 2

 Well, first we'll need a handsome prince, and a beautiful
 maiden, two ugly step sisters, a Fairy godm…

PUSS 'N BOOTS

 Blind Mice we are short on time. You are best to call each
 person's name generally one by one according to the
 script and assign a part.

BLIND MICE 1

 Of course, answer as I call you. Puss 'n Boots.

PUSS 'N BOOTS

 Ready. Name what part I am for.

BLIND MICE 2

 You, Puss 'n Boots, will play…

PUSS 'N BOOTS

 Prince Charming! Excellent choice my fine fellows –
 what is this prince, a lover or a fighter?

BLIND MICE 3

 A lover that kills himself, most gallant, for love.

PUSS 'N BOOTS

 Perfect, a true test, I will have the audience look into
 mine eyes, I will purr a little, and they will not be able to
 resist my charm. Although my preference is a fighter, I
 could be a swashbuckler, I would shout on guard. Then I
 would thrust parry thrust, thrust thrust parry parry, thrust
 – Salute! But still a lover is more condoling. Now name
 the rest of the players, and proceed.

BLIND MICE 1

 Troll, co-star of Three Billy Goats Gruff.

TROLL

 Here, Blind Mice.

BLIND MICE 2

You will play Cinderella.

TROLL

What is Cinderella? A wandering knight?

BLIND MICE 3

No, she is the lady that the prince falls in love with.

TROLL

Nay, faith, let me not play a woman: I have a beard
coming.

BLIND MICE 1

You must, can you see anyone else here who could play a
beautiful maiden? *(RAPUNZEL looks hopeful)* You will
wear this wig and speak in a very high voice.

*BLIND MICE 1 gives TROLL the end of RAPUNZEL'S hair as
wig.*

PUSS 'N BOOTS

A wig! Let me play Cinderella too, I could wear a wig
like in the French court and speak in a teeny tiny voice. I
would curtsy flutter curtsy, curtsy curtsy flutter flutter,
curtsy!

BLIND MICE 3

No, no; you must play Prince Charming and Troll you
Cinderella.

PUSS 'N BOOTS

Well proceed.

BLIND MICE 1

Prince Charming, star of Sleeping Beauty, Princess and
the Pea, Cinderella, and stunt double in the Frog Prince.

PRINCE CHARMING

Here, Blind Mice.

BLIND MICE 2
> You shall play Ugly Step Sister One.

BLIND MICE 1
> Rapunzel.

RAPUNZEL
> Here, Blind Mice.

BLIND MICE 2
> You shall play Ugly Step Sister Two.

BLIND MICE 2
> Straw man, you will play the lion's part.

BLIND MICE 3
> And we will be the lighting operators.

STRAW MAN
> Have you the lion's part written? Pray you, if it be, give it
> me; for I am slow of study.

BLIND MICE 3
> You may do it off the cuff, for it is nothing but roaring.

PUSS 'N BOOTS
> Roaring! Let me play the lion too. I will roar so loud that
> the king will say "let him roar again. Let him roar again!"

RAPUNZEL
> And you should do it too terribly, you would scare the
> ladies that they would shriek.

TROLL
> And that would be enough to have us all turned into
> toads.

ALL
> Aye, they'd turn us into toads, every mother's son.

PUSS 'N BOOTS

    I grant you, that if I scared the ladies out of their wits, they would have us all turned into toads. But I could roar as gently as a kitten. Meow. Meow.

BLIND MICE 3

    You can play no part but Prince Charming. Prince charming is a sweet-faced man, a handsome man, a gentlemanlike man.

PRINCE CHARMING

    Can I suggest that I…

BLIND MICE 1 (interrupts)

    Therefore, you must play the prince.

PUSS 'N BOOTS

    Well, I will undertake it. What boots were I best to play it in?

BLIND MICE 2

    Why, whatever pair you wish.

PUSS 'N BOOTS

    I could play it in my black gum boots, my red leather boots, my purple velvet boots or my blue suede shoes.

TROLL

    Your blue suede shoes are not boots at all and so you would play bootless.

BLIND MICE 1

    Masters, here are your parts, and I am to entreat you,

BLIND MICE 2

    Request you,

BLIND MICE 3

    And desire you, to learn them by tomorrow night.

BLIND MICE 2
> And meet us in the woods on the border of Candy Land.

BLIND MICE 3
> There we will rehearse in secret without interruptions.

PUSS 'N BOOTS
> We will meet, and there we will rehearse most obscenely and courageously. Take pains, be perfect. Adieu!

BLIND MICE 2
> See you tomorrow.

PUSS 'N BOOTS
> Enough! One for all and all for one.

ALL Exit.

SCENE 4 - THE WOODS

Enter CARDS 1-4. They are marching.

Enter PETER & PAN.

CARD 1
> How now spirits?

CARD 2
> Whither wander you?

PETER
> Over hill, over dale.

PAN
> Through bush, through briar.

PETER
> Over park, over pale.

PAN

      Through flood, through fire.

PETER & PAN

      We do wander everywhere,
      Swifter than the moon's sphere;
      And we do serve the Candy King.

CARD 1

      Unless we are mistaken you are those shrewd and knavish
      fellows, Peter & Pan.

CARD 3

      Are not you them?

CARD 4

      Tell us, please.

PETER

      Yes, you are right.

PAN

      We are those merry wanderers of the night.

PETER

      We jest to the Candy King and make him giggle.

PAN

      And perchance he'll give us a jelly squiggle.

PETER

      But hush, here comes our King.

CARD 2

      And her Majesty the Queen.

PETER, PAN & the CARDS bow.

Enter CANDY KING.
Enter QUEEN OF HEARTS, with her ACES.

CANDY KING
> Ill met by moonlight, Queen of Hearts.

QUEEN OF HEARTS
> What, jealous my King? Deck shuffle! I will not share
> my hand with this man.

*CARDS change positions with each other and stand behind
QUEEN.*

CANDY KING
> Tarry rash wonton. Am I not your lord?

QUEEN OF HEARTS
> Then I must be thy lady. But why then have I been
> discarded? You work day and night at the candy factory,
> while I am placed on the bottom of the pile.

CANDY KING
> I work hard to put chocolate on the table, but do you
> appreciate it? No.

QUEEN OF HEARTS
> Why should I? Every day I open the cupboard and all I
> find is sweets and candy.
>
> You know I cannot resist such temptation. Look at me!
> Before I meet you, I was thin as a card, the trump of the
> court, but now... I am as big as a deck.

PETER & PAN laugh.

QUEEN OF HEARTS
> Off with their heads!

CANDY KING
> No, no - please - I can't afford any more staff cuts. Look
> - these are the plans for my new factory.

CANDY KING gives the QUEEN OF HEARTS the plans.

CANDY KING
>All I need is hand full of cards to get started.

QUEEN OF HEARTS *(pushing away the plans.)*
>These are the forgeries of jellybeans. Even if I was the last card, I would have no part in such a deal. The working conditions in this factory are horrendous.

CANDY KING
>Why should my Queen cross her King? I do but beg a few cards to be my henchmen.

QUEEN OF HEARTS
>Set your heart at rest, for I will not part with them.

CANDY KING
>How long within my wood intend you to stay?

QUEEN OF HEARTS
>Perchance till after King Arthur's wedding day.

CANDY KING
>Give me the cards and I will go with you.

QUEEN OF HEARTS
>Not for thy Candy Kingdom. Cards away, pair, straight and march.

Exit QUEEN OF HEARTS, ACES & CARDS.

CANDY KING
>Go then. Peter, Pan come. Do you remember that delicious chocolate heart I once made?

PAN
>I remember.

PETER

> Yes, my lord.

CANDY KING

> Anyone who tastes its sweet chocolate shell and rich
> strawberry centre will fall in love with the next creature
> they see. Fetch me that chocolate delight from the vault.

PAN

> I'll put a girdle round about the earth.

PETER

> In forty minutes.

CANDY KING

> Just go get it.

PETER & PAN exit.

CANDY KING

> Once I have this treat,
> I'll watch my queen when she is asleep,
> And touch it to her lips.
> The next thing that she, waking, looks upon,
> Be it on lion, bear or wolf, or bull,
> On meddling monkey, or busy ape,
> She will fall madly in love with it.

> But who comes here? I will hide and see who it is.

Enter BIG BAD WOLF, with GOLDILOCKS chasing.

BIG BAD WOLF

> I like you not, therefore pursue me not. Where are Hansel
> and little Red Riding Hood? You told me they had gone
> into the woods, and for some reason that rang true, so I
> followed. But, where are they?

GOLDILOCKS

> What big eyes you have, what big ears you have, what big teeth you have.

BIG BAD WOLF

> Get thee gone and follow me no more. You are the woodcutter's daughter. He would have my head on his chopping block if he knew I was speaking to you.

GOLDILOCKS

> All I want is a little bit of fur for my new coat.

BIG BAD WOLF

> I will flee from thee.

Exit BIG BAD WOLF while GOLDILOCKS struggles with bolt of tranquilizer gun.

GOLDILOCKS

> Bother. Daddy's tranquilizer gun is harder to use than I thought.
> Run where you will, I'll follow you.

Exit GOLDILOCKS.

Enter PETER & PAN.

CANDY KING

> Do you have the box of chocolate hearts?

PETER

> Ay, here it is.

CANDY KING

> I pray thee give it me.

They hand him a box of chocolates.

> I know a bank where the wild thyme blows,
> Where oxlips and the nodding violet grows,

> There sleeps the queen sometime of the night,
> Lull'd in these flowers with dances and delight;
> And with this sweet, will I touch her lips.

PAN
> And she will fall in love with the next thing she sees.

CANDY KING
> Take this one. *(He gives PAN a chocolate)* Seek
> throughout this grove the companion of the sweet girl.
> You will know him by his big eyes, big ears and big teeth.
> Give it to him, so he shall be more fond of her.

PAN
> Fear not, my lord.

PETER
> Your servants shall do so.

Exit CANDY KING, PETER & PAN.

SCENE 5 - THE WOODS

Enter QUEEN OF HEARTS, ACES & CARDS.

QUEEN OF HEARTS
> Come, sing me now asleep. Then to your offices and let
> me rest.

ACE OF DIAMONDS
> You spotted snakes with double tongue,

ACE OF CLUBS
> Thorny hedgehogs, be not seen;

ACE OF SPADES
> Newts and blind-worms, do no wrong,

ACE OF HEARTS

       Come not near our fairy queen.

ACES & CARDS

       Philomel, with melody
       Sing in our sweet lullaby;
       Lulla, lulla, lullaby, lulla, lulla, lullaby:
       Never harm,
       Nor spell nor charm,
       Come our lovely lady nigh;
       So, good night, with lullaby.

ACE OF DIAMONDS

       Weaving spiders, come not here;

ACE OF CLUBS

       Hence, you long-legg'd spinners, hence!

ACE OF SPADES

       Beetles black, approach not near;

ACE OF HEARTS

       Worm nor snail, do no offence.

ACES & CARDS

       Philomel, with melody
       Sing in our sweet lullaby;
       Lulla, lulla, lullaby, lulla, lulla, lullaby:
       Never harm,
       Nor spell nor charm,
       Come our lovely lady nigh;
       So, good night, with lullaby.

QUEEN OF HEARTS sleeps.

ACE OF HEARTS

       Hence, away! Now all is well:
       We will now stand sentinel.

CARDS exit, ACES remain and guard the QUEEN.

Enter CANDY KING.

CANDY KING
Pssst.

ACE OF SPADES
What was that?

ACE OF DIAMONDS
Just the wind.

CANDY KING
Pssst. *(ACES look at the CANDY KING)* Would you like a lollypop?

ACES
Yes.

ACES exit happily licking their lollypops.

CANDY KING
What thou seest when thou dost wake,
Do it for thy true-love take,
Be it dog or cat or bear
Pig or boar with bristled hair.
When thou wakest, it is thy dear,
Wake when some vile thing is near.

CANDY KING touches the chocolate to QUEEN OF HEART'S lips then leaves.

Enter RED RIDING HOOD and HANSEL.

HANSEL
Fair love, you are faint vith vandering in the vood, and to tell you zhe truth, I think ve are lost. Maybe ve should rest here for a vhile.

RED RIDING HOOD
I am tired. I will lie down on this grassy moss.

RED RIDING HOOD pulls out a sleeping mask, and wraps her cape around her.

Good night.

RED RIDING HOOD sleeps.

HANSEL
Guten Nacht.

HANSEL sleeps. PETER & PAN appear from behind a tree.

PAN
Who is here?

PETER
This must be who our master meant,
For here's the maiden, sleeping sound,
On the dank and dirty ground.

PAN
Big eyes, big ears, and big teeth?
Yes, this must be him.

PAN feeds sweet to HANSEL. PETER & PAN exit.

Enter GOLDILOCKS and BIG BAD WOLF.

GOLDILOCKS
Stay still, so I can shoot you, my little wolf.

BIG BAD WOLF
Why do you hunt me thus? Leave me alone.

*GOLDILOCKS aims gun at the BIG BAD WOLF as he flees,
shoots and misses.
Exit BIG BAD WOLF.*

GOLDILOCKS

> O, I am out of breath in this fond chase!
> The more my prayer, the lesser is my grace.

GOLDILOCKS sees HANSEL sleeping.

> But who is here? Hansel on the ground.

GOLDILOCKS puts her gun on the ground as she crouches beside him.

> Dead or asleep? I see no blood, no wound. I hope I did not hit him with that stray shot.
>
> Hansel if you live, good sir awake.

HANSEL *(Awaking)*

> And run through fire I vill for thy sveet sake. Goldilocks, my love! Vhere is the volf? If only your father had cleaved him in two.

GOLDILOCKS

> Do not say so Hansel, say not so.
> It would surely damage his hide you know.
> Anyway, your love Red Riding Hood is safe and sound.
> Be content.

HANSEL

> Nein, I do repent the tedious minutes I vith her have spent.
> Not Red Riding Hood but Goldilocks do I love. Prick me with your dart my love, skin me, stuff me, take me to your taxidermist!

GOLDILOCKS

> Wherefore was I to this keen mockery born?
> When at your hands did I deserve such scorn?
> Besides - I am a collector of fine and rare animal hides. I am not interested your leather clad rump.

Exit GOLDILOCKS.

HANSEL
> Vait Goldilocks! I know vhere a cottage is made of gingerbread and candy.

Exit HANSEL following GOLDILOCKS.

RED RIDING HOOD stirs.

RED RIDING HOOD
> Help me, Hansel, help me. The wolf is chasing me, help me! *(she wakes)* Ay me, for pity! What a dream was here! Hansel look how I do quake with fear. I thought I was lost in the woods with the Big Bad Wolf. Hansel? My love, gone? What's this? A gun? What has happened here?

RED RIDING HOOD picks up GOLDILOCKS'S gun.

> Hansel, where are you? Hansel!

RED RIDING HOOD spies something on the ground.

> A trail of bread crumbs? I will find you my love. I will find you.

RED RIDING HOOD places gun in her basket, and exits following the trail.

SCENE 6 - THE WOODS

Enter 3 BLIND MICE, STRAW MAN, PUSS 'N BOOTS, TROLL, PRINCE CHARMING, & RAPUNZEL.

PUSS 'N BOOTS
> Are we all here?

BLIND MICE 1
> *(Taps the ground with his stick)* This looks like a
> marvellous convenient place for our rehearsal.

PRINCE CHARMING
> This shall be our stage-

RAPUNZEL
> These fine people our audience.

BLIND MICE 2
> And we will do it in action as we would before the King.

PUSS 'N BOOTS
> Blind Mice!

BLIND MICE 3
> What say'st thou, Puss 'n Boots?

PUSS 'N BOOTS
> There are things in this tragedy of Prince Charming and
> Cinderella that just will not do. First, Cinderella must lose
> her shoe and flee bare foot from the castle. This I cannot
> abide, what say you to this?

TROLL
> Oh no, I might get a stone bruise.

RAPUNZEL
> I believe she must leave her shoes on, when all is done.

PUSS 'N BOOTS
> Never fear, I have a plan. We will use a shoe double, and
> we will leave it on the steps and we shall have a prologue
> to explain that Cinderella has fled the scene and no nasty
> toes need be seen.

BLIND MICE 2
> Well, we will have such a shoe double and let it be a size
> 6.

PUSS 'N BOOTS
No, make it two more, let it be a size 8.

BLIND MICE 3
Let it be so.

STRAW MAN
Will not the ladies be afraid of the lion?

TROLL
I fear it, I promise you.

PUSS 'N BOOTS
Blind mice. Have you read the script? *(BLIND MICE shake their heads)* Masters, I assure you there is no lion in the tale of Cinderella. So, we need not look into it.

TROLL
There is a pumpkin that turns into a carriage.

PRINCE CHARMING
Therefore, another prologue must explain the pumpkin is not a pumpkin.

PUSS 'N BOOTS
Yes, we will place the pumpkin on the steps and say "ladies" or "fair ladies", I would have you know or understand or perceive that this pumpkin is not a pumpkin but is a carriage, that was a pumpkin.

BLIND MICE 1
Well, then it shall be so.

RAPUNZEL
But there is another challenging thing. Cinderella flees the dance at midnight - but how will the audience know it is midnight?

STRAW MAN

>Is the play on at midnight?

PUSS 'N BOOTS

>A program, a program, look in the program. Is it
>midnight? Is it midnight?

They all crowd around and read the program.

RAPUNZEL

>No, it starts at seven.

PRINCE CHARMING

>Why, then we shall pretend it's midnight.

STRAW MAN

>Aye, or else one must come with a clock and bell and say
>he comes to represent the time.

ALL

>Aye. That's a good idea. Yes. *(and so on)*

BLIND MICE 2

>Then there is another thing. There has to be a ball, for the
>story says Prince Charming and Cinderella did meet at a
>ball.

BLIND MICE 3

>We can't throw a ball.

BLIND MICE 1

>It's not in the budget.

RAPUNZEL

>What say you Puss 'n Boots?

PUSS 'N BOOTS *(pauses to think deeply)*

>Some man or other must represent "Ball": And let him be
>dressed appropriately with gold and wig. And let him play

a tune to which Prince Charming and Cinderella can
dance.

BLIND MICE 1

Then all is well. Come sit down and rehearse your parts.

BLIND MICE 2

Prince Charming you begin. When you have spoken your
speech enter into that brake and so everyone according to
your cue.

Enter PETER & PAN. They clap hands and actors freeze.

PETER

What ragtag bunch have we loitering here?

PAN

So near the cradle of the Queen of Hearts.

PETER

What - a play toward!

PAN

I will be a director.

PETER

An actor too perhaps, if I see cause.

PAN

Action! *(Clap hands)*

BLIND MICE 2

Speak Prince Charming. Cinderella, get ready.

PUSS 'N BOOTS

Send soiled invites to the ball…

BLIND MICE 3

Royal, royal.

PUSS 'N BOOTS

> Send royal invites to the ball,
> Let every lady hear my call.
> From servant girl to maiden fair,
> So at them all, I may glare.

Exit PUSS 'N BOOTS.

PAN

> I think I will go hound this prince.

Exit PAN.

TROLL *(nervously)*

> Must I speak now?

BLIND MICE 1

> Yes. You must understand the invitation has arrived
> asking you to the ball, where you are to meet the prince.

TROLL

> Oh, look a royal invite in gold and purple hues,
> And all I have upon my feet are these dirty shoes.
> Fairy Godmother, please help me in my lone distress,
> And make for me a brand new super sparkly pretty dress.
> I hope the prince will notice me, from right across the
> tomb.

BLIND MICE 3

> Room, not tomb. But you do not say that yet, first you go
> to the ball and Prince Charming enters and sees you.

BLIND MICE 2

> You speak all your part at once.

BLIND MICE 3

> Prince, enter! Your cue is past. It was "pretty dress."

TROLL
>   Oh, "And make for me a brand new super sparkly pretty
>   dress."

PUSS 'N BOOTS enters wearing a leash with a dog's head. Enter
PAN who joins PETER to watch the scene unfold.

PUSS 'N BOOTS
>   O grim looked night, O night with hue so black,

BLIND MICE 1
>   I smell a hound.

BLIND MICE 2
>   Beware!

BLIND MICE 3
>   Dog!

BLIND MICE 1
>   Run!

BLIND MICE 2
>   Flee!

BLIND MICE 3
>   Help!

Exit THREE BLIND MICE.

PRINCE CHARMING
>   Three blind mice?

RAPUNZEL
>   Three blind mice!

STRAW MAN
>   See how they run.

TROLL
>See how they run!

PRINCE CHARMING *(Pointing at PUSS 'N BOOTS)*
>Have you ever see such a thing in your life?

ALL except PUSS 'N BOOTS
>Ahh, three blind mice!

STRAW MAN, PRINCE CHARMING & TROLL exit at a run.
RAPUNZEL faints.

PUSS 'N BOOTS
>Why do they run away? Is it midnight already? I thought
>the ball had just started?

Enter PRINCE CHARMING to assists RAPUNZEL.

PRINCE CHARMING
>Puss? You have been turned astray!

PUSS 'N BOOTS
>What do you mean?

RAPUNZEL
>Bless you Puss, you have been transformed!

Exit PRINCE CHARMING & RAPUNZEL.

PUSS 'N BOOTS
>I see their game. They are trying to scare me, if they
>could, by leaving me alone in the woods. I will remain
>here. In fact, I am glad to be no longer dogged by their
>company. How can one be afraid when the moon shines
>so bright? I will sing and they will hear I am not fearful.
>*(Howls at moon)*
>
>Hey diddle diddle, (howl, howl)
>The cat and the fiddle, (howl, howl)

The cow jumped over the moon,

QUEEN OF HEARTS
What angel wakes me from my flowery bed?

PUSS 'N BOOTS
The little dog laughed to see such fun,
And the dish ran away with the spoon. (howl, howl)

PUSS 'N BOOTS continues to howl.

QUEEN OF HEARTS
I pray you, gentle puppy, sing again,
Mine ear is much enamoured of thy note,
So is mine eye enthralled to thy shape,
Oh, you are so cute, oh I just love you.

PUSS 'N BOOTS
I think, my lady, your puppy love is mistaken, for I am
not canine but rather feline.

QUEEN OF HEARTS
You are both wise and beautiful.

PUSS 'N BOOTS
Thank you, my lady, now if you would be so kind as to
point me in the right direction. I wish to leave these
woods.

*PUSS 'N BOOTS tries to leave but the QUEEN grabs hold of the
leash.*

QUEEN OF HEARTS
Out of these woods do not desire to go. Thou shalt remain
here whether thou wilt or no. For I am Her Majesty, the
Queen of Hearts.

PUSS 'N BOOTS
My Queen. *(He bows)* I have long desired to visit you.

QUEEN OF HEARTS
>Welcome then. This is my domain and I do love thee.
>Come with me and I shall show you my hand, the aces of
>my court. They will feed you, groom you, pamper you
>and polish your boots. Hearts, Diamonds, Spades and
>Clubs.

Enter ACES.

ACE OF HEARTS
>Ready,

ACE OF DIAMONDS
>And I,

ACE OF SPADES
>And I,

ACE OF CLUBS
>And I,

ALL ACES
>Your Majesty. (Bowing)

QUEEN OF HEARTS
>Be kind and courteous to this gentleman. Serve him and
>care for him.

ACE OF HEARTS
>My lord, welcome.

ACE OF DIAMONDS
>Welcome.

ACE OF SPADES
>Welcome.

ACE OF CLUBS
>Welcome.

PUSS 'N BOOTS
> Why what a fine pack of suitors you are. *(to ACE OF HEARTS)* Your name, good sir.

ACE OF HEARTS
> Ace of Hearts.

PUSS 'N BOOTS
> Good to meet you Ace of Hearts, if I have need of a coronary bypass. I will call on you.
> *(to ACE OF SPADES)* Your name, good sir.

ACE OF SPADES *(Bowing)*
> Ace of Spades.

PUSS 'N BOOTS
> Ace of Spades, I will call on you if I need to bury a bone.

ACE OF DIAMONDS *(Bowing)*
> Ace of Diamonds.

PUSS 'N BOOTS
> Ace of Diamonds, I will call on you if I become so bold as to ask the queen's hand in marriage.

ACE OF CLUBS *(Bowing)*
> Ace of Clubs.

PUSS 'N BOOTS
> Why, I was quite a dancer in my disco days.

QUEEN OF HEARTS
> Come, wait on him. Lead him to my left bower.

ALL Exit.

INTERVAL

SCENE 6 - THE WOODS

Enter JESTER, COURTIER & 3 LITTLE PIGS.

JESTER

As you are all aware, the King has allowed amateurs to enter the competition.

Now, as a professional theatre company, we are not going to let a bunch of amateur show us up, are we?

3 LITTLE PIGS & COURTIER
No Sir, No!

JESTER

So, we are going to do the last scene until we get it absolutely perfect. Do you understand? I want to feel it! I want to be blown away!

3 LITTLE PIGS & COURTIER,
Yes Sir!

JESTER

To your places. And action!

COURTIER *(as Big Bad Wolf)*
Little pig, little pig let me in.

LITTLE PIG 1
Not by the hair on my chinny chin chin.

COURTIER
Then I'll huff and I'll puff and I will blow your house in.

COURTIER blows, LITTLE PIG 1 runs over to LITTLE PIG 2.

COURTIER *(as Big Bad wolf)*
Little pig, little pig let me in.

LITTLE PIG 2
>Not by the hair on my chinny chin chin.

JESTER
>Wait, give me more huff, more puff this time. Like this.

JESTER demonstrates

>Then I'll huff and I'll puff and I will blow your house in!

JESTER blows, LITTLE PIG 1 & LITTLE PIG 2 run over to LITTLE PIG 3.

JESTER
>Now you try it.

COURTIER *(as Big Bad Wolf)*
>Little pig, little pig let me in.

LITTLE PIG 3
>Not by the hair on my chinny chin chin.

COURTIER
>Then I'll huff and I'll puff and I will blow your house in.

COURTIER blows but the 3 LITTLE PIGS just stand there with their hands on the hips.

JESTER
>Yes, yes superb! I want to feel the voraciousness. Taste the fear! Ok… let's go work on our costumes.

ALL Exit.

SCENE 8 - THE WOODS

Enter CANDY KING.

CANDY KING
>I wonder what the queen did see when she awoke?

Enter PETER & PAN laughing.

> Here comes Peter & Pan. How now, boys. Tell me all that
> has happened.

PETER

> The Queen

PAN

> -with a monster-

PETER

> is in love.

CANDY KING

> This falls out better than I could devise. Tell me all that
> transpired.

PAN

> Near to her close and consecrated bower,
> While she was in her dull and sleeping hour,

PETER

> A crew of cliché characters did rehearse a play,

PAN

> Intended for King Arthur's wedding day.

PETER

> There one "Puss 'n Boots" did play Prince Charming.

PAN

> And when he exited stage left, I followed and turned him
> into a dog.

PETER

> When he returned his fellow cast fled, leaving this now
> "Mutt 'n Boots" alone.

PAN

> At this moment, the Queen awoke and fell in love with
> the flea bag.

CANDY KING

> Excellent. Did you also give the chocolate heart to the
> other fellow, as I instructed?

PETER

> We found him sleeping and did give him the sweet treat.

CANDY KING

> Silence. Here he comes.

Enter RED RIDING HOOD & BIG BAD WOLF.

PAN

> This is the girl but I have not seen this wolf before.

RED RIDING HOOD (*crying*)

> Hansel, Hansel!

RED RIDING HOOD looks up and sees the BIG BAD WOLF.

> Wicked, evil wolf thou hast eaten him,
> So should a murderer look, so dead, so grim.

BIG BAD WOLF

> Yuck, I would not eat him; those leather pants are too
> tough and chewy. But you, sweet little girl, I will happily
> gobble up.

RED RIDING HOOD

> Out dog! Freeze wolf! *(Pulls GOLDILOCK's gun)* I am
> past the bounds of a maiden's patience. If you did not eat
> Hansel, then where is he? Tell me the truth.

BIG BAD WOLF

> I have not eaten him, nor is he dead for all that I can tell.

RED RIDING HOOD
I pray thee, tell me then that he is well.

BIG BAD WOLF
Put down the gun and I will tell you.

RED RIDING HOOD
Stay back liar! You do not know where he is. This is the last you will see of me.

She *shoots a dart, it strikes BIG BAD WOLF in the side. RED RIDING HOOD exits.*

BIG BAD WOLF
There is no following her with this dart in my vein.
Here therefore for a while I will remain.
So sleepy. *(Falls asleep, snoring)*

CANDY KING
What hast thou done?

PETER & PAN
Oops.

CANDY KING
Fly quickly and find the girl Goldilocks and bring her here.

PETER
I go, I go, look how I go!

PAN
Swifter than an arrow from Cupid's bow.

Exit PETER & PAN.

CANDY KING gives sweet to BIG BAD WOLF.

CANDY KING

> What thou see'st when thou dost wake,
> Do it for thy true love take.

Enter PETER & PAN.

PETER

> Captain of the Candyland.

PAN

> Goldilocks is here at hand.

PETER

> And the youth mistook by us.

PAN

> Following her with quite a fuss.

CANDY KING

> Stand aside, the noise that they make
> Will surely cause the Wolf to wake.

PETER

> Then two strange creatures will love one.

PAN

> Well done good sir, this should be fun.

Enter HANSEL and GOLDILOCKS.

HANSEL *(Rubbing the rump of his lederhosen)*

> I assure you, it is A grade leather, durable, easy to clean
> and oh, so snug fitting. Wundabar.

GOLDILOCKS

> I am not interested in your lederhosen. Besides, are you
> not planning to wear them when you wed little Red
> Riding Hood?

HANSEL

Nein, I vill not marry her, the Volf can have her. Anyvay, I have a spare pair.

GOLDILOCKS

A curse on both your trousers.

BIG BAD WOLF *(wakes and sees GOLDILOCKS)*

Goldilocks fair huntress, I submit,
My heart is pierced by your dart.
Use me but as your spaniel; spurn me, strike me,
Neglect me, lose me; only give me leave,
Unworthy as I am, to follow you.

GOLDILOCKS

Do you mock me? I see you all are bent
To set against me for your merriment.

GOLDILOCKS notices the dart in his hide.

I fired no weapon. Yet this is my dart. Someone else has poached my trophy!

BIG BAD WOLF

Red Riding Hood may have fired the shot, but it is your dart that protrudes from my rump.

HANSEL

Get avay from her, you hairy heap of road kill. You belong to Red Riding Hood according to section 43 of the Fairy Land Hunting Code.

GOLDILOCKS

That little minx.

BIG BAD WOLF

Hansel, look here comes your love.

Enter RED RIDING HOOD.

RED RIDING HOOD
>   Hansel there you are, why did you leave me?

HANSEL
>   Let go of me. I no longer vant to take you to my candy cottage.

RED RIDING HOOD
>   What do you mean?

HANSEL
>   I am taking fair Goldilocks instead. Now, go avay.

RED RIDING HOOD
>   Goldilocks? I do not understand.

GOLDILOCKS
>   You poaching little scarlet harlot. Do not act so innocent! You steal my gun, shoot my prize, and now you return to claim his hide.

RED RIDING HOOD
>   What are you talking about?

GOLDILOCKS
>   Oh, innocent little Red Riding Hood. You knew, when you shot the Big Bad Wolf, all other claims on the trophy are null and void.

HANSEL
>   Calm down my love. You still have me.

GOLDILOCKS
>   O, Wunderbar.

RED RIDING HOOD
>   Hansel why do you tease her?

BIG BAD WOLF *(to GOLDILOCKS)*
>   Forget the code, I am yours.

HANSEL *(pushing BIG BAD WOLF aside)*
> Back cur! Zhe rules are zhe rules. *(To GOLDILOCKS)*
> Now, how about a leather jacket?

BIG BAD WOLF
> No, a fur coat.

HANSEL
> Stand back foul beast.

BIG BAD WOLF
> Make your move, Fritz.

RED RIDING HOOD *(Stepping between them.)*
> Stop!

HANSEL
> Away you vench.

BIG BAD WOLF
> Hiding behind a girl.

HANSEL
> Let go of my arm you monochromatic hussy!

RED RIDING HOOD
> But…. I thought you liked red?

HANSEL
> Like it? I despise it. Now it is gold zhat I adore.

RED RIDING HOOD *(to GOLDILOCKS)*
> Why you porridge pilfering harlequin! Will you steal my
> Hansel too?

GOLDILOCKS
> What did you call me? I am going to rip that red cap to
> shreds.

RED RIDING HOOD
> Not before I tear out those golden locks.

HANSEL *(Stepping forward to protect GOLDILOCKS)*
> Do not be afraid. She vill not harm you, fair maiden.

GOLDILOCKS
> Get out of my way, I can defend myself. I know Kung Fu.

BIG BAD WOLF
> Stand aside!

HANSEL
> I challenge you to a duel!

BIG BAD WOLF
> I accept, lead the way.

Exit BIG BAD WOLF and HANSEL.

GOLDILOCKS
> Now, where were we?

RED RIDING HOOD
> Ah, Kung Fu, I think. But I know how to skip, which is a very efficient way to flee.

Exit RED RIDING HOOD, leaves her basket containing the tranquilizer gun.

GOLDILOCKS
> You chicken! Get back here.

Exit GOLDILOCKS.

The CANDY KING turns to PETER & PAN.

CANDY KING

> This is thy negligence. Was it a mistake or did you do it on purpose?

PAN

> A mistake, your majesty we assure you.

PETER

> Did not you tell us, we would know him for his big eyes, big ears, and big teeth?

PAN

> We are blameless my lord, for many would make such a mistake.

CANDY KING

> Take this *(gives PAN tranquilizer gun)* and hunt them down before they tear each other apart. Once they are sedated give this mint to Hansel, it will break the love spell. Meanwhile, I will find the Queen of Hearts and release her from the charm.

Exit CANDY KING.

PETER

> Up and down, up and down,
> We will lead them round and round.

PAN

> All the way through field and town,
> We will lead them up and down,
>
> Here comes one now.

Enter HANSEL.

HANSEL

> Vhere art thou Volf? Speak, so I can find you in zhis darkness.

PAN *(in the BIG BAD WOLF's voice)*
>   I'll huff and I'll puff and I'll blow your house in.

HANSEL
>   I have you now foul beast.

PAN
>   Follow me to open ground.

Exit HANSEL. Enter BIG BAD WOLF.

BIG BAD WOLF
>   Hansel, speak! The coward has run away. Speak, where
>   are you hiding?

PETER *(in HANSEL's voice)*
>   Oh look, a gingerbread cottage made of sveets and candy.
>   My favourite.

BIG BAD WOLF
>   Now I have you.

PETER
>   Follow my voice.

Exit BIG BAD WOLF. Enter HANSEL.

HANSEL
>   Unbelievable, I am lost again, I cannot find zhis foe, I
>   follow his voice but he is never zhere. *(PAN shoots
>   HANSEL)* Achtung! Oh, look at all the pretty colours.
>   *(Sleeps)*

BIG BAD WOLF
>   Boy, I grow weary of this chase, come out and face me
>   like a man. *(PAN shoots BIG BAD WOLF who howls)*
>   Not agaaaaaaainnnnnn…

BIG BAD WOLF sleeps. Enter RED RIDING HOOD.

RED RIDING HOOD
>Never so weary, never so in woe,
>I can no further skip, no further go.

PAN shoots RED RIDING HOOD.

RED RIDING HOOD
>Ouch!

RED RIDING HOOD sleeps.

PETER
>Yet but three? Come one more,

PAN
>Two of both kinds make up four,

Enter GOLDILOCKS.

GOLDILOCKS
>O weary night! O long and tedious night
>I cannot find her tracks in this low light.

PETER PAN shoots GOLDILOCKS

>Oh, suddenly so sleepy. I will lay my head upon this rock.
>Oh, no this one is too hard,
>This one is too soft,
>Ah, this one is just right. *(Sleeps)*

PETER
>On the ground,
>Sleep sound.

PAN *(gives Hansel mint)*
>When you wake, you will once again love little Red
>Riding Hood.

PETER & PAN *(Sing as they leave)*
>Jack and Jill went up the hill to fetch a pale of water.
>Jack fell down and broke his crown and Jill come
>tumbling after.

Exit PETER & PAN.

SCENE 9 - THE WOODS

*Enter QUEEN OF HEART & ACES with PUSS 'N BOOTS on a
dog's leash.*

QUEEN OF HEARTS
>Come. Heel, now sit. Lie down, good boy.

PUSS 'N BOOTS
>Where's the Ace of Hearts?

ACE OF HEARTS
>Ready.

PUSS 'N BOOTS
>Scratch my head, Monsieur Hearts. Where is the Ace of
>Clubs?

ACE OF CLUBS
>Ready.

PUSS 'N BOOTS
>Monsieur clubs, good Monsieur, get your weapons in
>your hand and bludgeon me a wild ass and good
>Monsieur bring me the leg bone. And Monsieur, have a
>care not to break the bone as I desire to chew on it. Where
>is the Ace of Diamonds?

ACE OF DIAMONDS
>Ready.

PUSS 'N BOOTS
> Good Monsieur Diamonds.

ACE OF DIAMONDS
> What's your will?

PUSS 'N BOOTS
> Nothing, good Monsieur but to help Hearts scratch.
> Methinks, I am dogged by fleas.

QUEEN OF HEARTS
> Will you hear some music my sweet love?

PUSS 'N BOOTS
> I have a reasonable good ear for music. I once played a
> fiddle, perhaps I could sing along,
> Hey diddle diddle,
> The cat and the fiddle,
> The cow -

QUEEN OF HEARTS *(Interrupts)*
> Or say, sweet love, perhaps you desire something to eat?

PUSS 'N BOOTS
> I could munch on a good dry biscuit. Methinks, I have a
> great desire for a large roll of sausage. Good sausage,
> sweet sausage, hath no fellow.

QUEEN OF HEARTS
> I could have some cards fetch you a bowl of peanuts?

PUSS 'N BOOTS
> I would rather a bone. But, I pray you, *(yawns)* let none of
> your people stir me, I have an exposition of sleep come
> upon me.

QUEEN OF HEARTS
> Cards discard. *(Exit ACES.)*
> Sleep thou, and I will wind thee in my arms.
> O, how I love thee! How I dote on thee!

They Sleep.

Enter PETER & PAN. CANDY KING comes forward.

CANDY KING
> Welcome, good Peter, good Pan. See'st thou this sweet
> sight? She is in love with a hound. Yet I begin to pity her.
> The enchantment has caused her to forget our quarrel.
> When I again requested a pack of cards to work in the
> new jellybean forge, she sent them without question. Now
> I have the workers I require, I will undo the spell.

Gives QUEEN OF HEARTS a mint.

> Wake, my sweet Queen.

QUEEN OF HEARTS   *(waking)*
> My Lord, what visions have I seen?
> Methought I was enamoured of a dog.

CANDY KING
> There lies your love.

QUEEN OF HEARTS (*getting up with a cry of surprise*).
> Oh, I am so not a dog person, far too high maintenance.

CANDY KING
> Pan, remove the leash from this feline, so he may return
> to his fairy tale fellows.

PAN
> Now, when you wake with your own feline eyes peep.

PAN removes leash and dog head.

PETER
> Candy King, gone is the dark,
> I do hear the morning lark.

CANDY KING
> Then my queen, let us depart,
> For a royal wedding is about to start,

QUEEN OF HEARTS
> Come, my lord, and in our flight
> Tell me how it came this night
> That I sleeping here was found
> With this dog upon the ground?

Exit CANDY KING, QUEEN OF HEARTS, PETER & PAN.

Enter COURTIER.

COURTIER
> Presenting, his Majesty, King Arthur of Fairyland and his
> royal bride, Lady Guinevere.

Enter KING ARTHUR, GUINEVERE, WICKED STEPMOTHER and CAPTIAN.

KING ARTHUR
> My Queen have you enjoyed the hunt this fine morning?

GUINEVERE
> I have my lord, it has been most enjoyable. I am glad you
> asked me to come.

KING ARTHUR
> Wait, who is it that lies here?

WICKED STEPMOTHER
> My Lord, this is my step daughter here asleep,
> And this Hansel; this the Big Bad Wolf;
> This Goldilocks the woodcutter's daughter;
> I wonder of their being here together?

GUINEVERE
> No doubt they rose up early to see the hunt.

KING ARTHUR
>Speak Wicked Step Mother; is not this the day
>That Red Riding hood should give answer of her choice?

WICKED STEPMOTHER
>It is, my lord.

KING ARTHUR
>Captain of the Guard, awake them.

CAPTAIN wakes them from their slumber. RED RIDING HOOD, HANSEL, BIG BAD WOLF & GOLDILOCKS wake up.

HANSEL
>My Lord.

KING ARTHUR
>Stand up. I know you two are rival enemies:
>How comes this gentle peace?

HANSEL
>Half sleep, half vaking; but as yet I svear,
>I cannot truly say how I came here.
>I zhink, I ran avay vith Red Riding Hood,
>Our intent vas to hide from her, *(points to Wicked Mother)* if ve could.

WICKED STEPMOTHER
>Enough! Enough – my lord you have enough!
>I beg the law, the law enforced.
>Lock her in a tower or feed her, er... wed her to the Wolf.

BIG BAD WOLF
>My Lord, fair Goldilocks told me of their plan to go into the woods. And I in gluttony did follow them. Fair Goldilocks, in fancy following me. But I do not know why but my desire for Red Riding Hood has melted away. It is now my pleasure to belong to Goldilocks.

GOLDILOCKS

And I would have him, my Lord but it is impossible. Red Riding Hood shot him with my gun, so now I have no legal claim.

CAPTAIN OF THE GUARD

Is the gun registered in your family name?

GOLDILOCKS

Yes, it is.

CAPTAIN OF THE GUARD

Well, then according to the Fairy Land Hunting Code you do have a claim under the misuse of a weapon registered in another's name.

KING ARTHUR

Very well, it is settled then.

Turns to Wicked Stepmother.

Wicked Step Mother your preferred son in law has declined, leaving Red Riding Hood to do as she pleases. Goldilocks, your claim on the wolf stands, he is your property.

Now I invite you all to join our wedding celebrations. Come Guinevere.

Exit KING ARTHUR, GUINEVERE, WICKED STEPMOTHER, COURTIER and CAPTAIN.

BIG BAD WOLF

My head is still a bit cloudy; did he say I am legally yours?

GOLDILOCKS

Mine, all mine.

HANSEL
>Come let us all go to zhe palace together.

RED RIDING HOOD *(to GOLDILOCKS)*
>I love weddings. What are you going to wear?

GOLDILOCKS
>Oh, I have something special in mind.

Exit GOLDILOCKS, BIG BAD WOLF, HANSEL & RED RIDING HOOD.

PUSS 'N BOOTS
>*(Dreaming)* When my cue comes, call me, and I will answer. My next is "Most fair prince".

PUSS 'N BOOTS wakes.

>On guard! Blind mice? Troll? Prince Charming? Rapunzel? God's my life! Stolen hence and left me asleep!

>I have had a most rare vision. I have had a dream past the wit of man to say what dream it was. Man is but a fool if he go about to explain this dream. Methought I was – there is no man can tell what. Methought I was and methought I wore, but man is dog's best friend if he dared to say what methought I wore. The eye of man hath not heard, the ear of man hath not seen, man's hand is not able to taste, his tongue to conceive, nor his heart to report, what my dream was.

>I will get the Blind Mice to write a ballad of this dream: it shall be called Puss's Dream, because no man can explain it; and I will sing it in the latter end of a play, before the King. Peradventure, to make it the more gracious, I shall sing it at her death.

Exit PUSS 'N BOOTS.

SCENE 10 - THE TOWN

Enter 3 BLIND MICE, PRINCE CHARMING, TROLL & STRAW MAN.

BLIND MICE 1
>Have you seen Puss 'n Boots? Has he come back yet?

PRINCE CHARMING
>He cannot be found. No doubt he is forever lost.

TROLL
>If he does not come then the play is over. It goes not forward. Does it?

BLIND MICE 2
>It is not possible. We have not another in all fairyland able to discharge Prince Charming but he.

PRINCE CHARMING
>Well I suppose I could…

BLIND MICE 3 *(interrupts)*
>No, he has simply the best wit of any fairy tale character.

PRINCE CHARMING
>But perhaps…

STRAW MAN *(interrupts)*
>Yes, and the best fellow too.

PRINCE CHARMING
>I really…

TROLL
>And he has such a purr to his sweet voice.

PRINCE CHARMING sighs.

Enter RAPUNZEL.

RAPUNZEL

> Masters, the king has come from the church with his
> guests. If our play had gone forward, we all would have
> been made stars.

TROLL

> O sweet Puss 'n Boots. He could have afforded new boots
> every day for the rest of his life. For if the king had not
> given him a new pair of boots each day for playing Prince
> Charming, I'll be turned to stone.

STRAW MAN

> He would have deserved it.

TROLL

> A new pair of boots each day or nothing.

Enter PUSS 'N BOOTS.

PUSS 'N BOOTS

> Hello lads. Did someone say new boots?

BLIND MICE 1

> Puss!

BLIND MICE 2

> O most courageous day!

BLIND MICE 3

> O most happy hour!

PUSS 'N BOOTS

> Masters, I have had some adventure, but ask me not about
> it, for I would not boast of my prowess. Ok, I will tell you
> everything. I was fabulous.

RAPUNZEL

> Let us hear, sweet Puss.

PUSS 'N BOOTS

> No, not a word of me. All I will tell you is the king has
> dined. Get together your costumes, string up your boots,
> put ribbons in your hair, and meet me at the palace every
> man in character. For the long and short of it is our play
> has been shortlisted. Let Cinderella get her dress, and
> Straw man fetch his pumpkin. And, most dear actors, eat
> no onions nor garlic, for we are to utter sweet breath and I
> do not doubt but to hear them say, it is a sweet tragedy.
> No more words, away. Go, away!

Exit All.

SCENE 11 - KING ARTHUR'S COURT

Enter COURTIER, CAPTAIN & WICKED STEPMOTHER.

WICKED STEPMOTHER

> Captain, are you absolutely sure about that hunting law?
> Perhaps you were mistaken?

CAPTAIN

> No, Madam. The rules of Fairyland are clear and must be
> obeyed.

WICKED STEPMOTHER

> Very well then, of course. *(Smiles crookedly)* What a
> noble young man you are. So hard working. You must be
> quite hungry. *(She brings out an apple from within her
> cloak)* Apple?

CAPTAIN

> I don't think so.

Trumpet sounds.

COURTIER
>Presenting the King of Fairyland and his bride, her
>Majesty, Queen Guinevere.

Enter GUINEVERE and KING ARTHUR.

GUINEVERE
>Oh Arthur, it is a strange story they speak of.

KING ARTHUR
>Such a fairy tale cannot be true.

GUINEVERE
>Yes, but they all declare it is.

KING ARTHUR
>Good Wicked Stepmother, what do you make of it all?

WICKED STEPMOTHER
>I will be speaking to the German Embassy about this.

COURTIER
>Presenting Hansel & Red Riding Hood.

Enter HANSEL & RED RIDING HOOD.

>Presenting Goldilocks & the Big Bad Wolf.

*Enter GOLDILOCKS & BIG BAD WOLF. GOLDILOCKS is
wearing a new fur coat, and the BIG BAD WOLF is in one-piece
pyjamas.*

Everyone gasps, and then laughs.

CAPTAIN OF THE GUARD
>A Toast to the King and Queen!

ALL
>Hooray!

KING ARTHUR

    Now where is our usual manager of mirth? Is there no play to entertain us? Call the court Jester.

Enter JESTER.

JESTER

    Here I am, your majesty.

KING ARTHUR

    What plays are preferred?

JESTER *(hands him a scroll)*

    Why here is a short list of plays. Pick as you please, my lord. Though I would suggest the ones at the top.

KING ARTHUR

    Hmm let me see.

    (Reads) "Snow White, the Handsome Dwarf and his 6 Ugly Brothers" by Grumpy Dwarf.

    No none of that, I have heard it is a monologue.

    (Reads) "The Tall Tale of Tom Thumb"

GUINEVERE

    I've already seen that one.

KING ARTHUR

    Hmm... what is this? *(Reads)* The Royal Jester Company presents 'MacBear'?

JESTER

    It is highly recommended, my lord.

GUINEVERE

    Let us see a preview my dear.

JESTER claps his hands, enter THREE BEARS with a large pot.

FIRST BEAR
>Thrice the morning cock has crowed.

SECOND BEAR
>Thrice has the alarm clock chimed.

THIRD BEAR
>It is time, it is time, it is porridge time.

FIRST BEAR
>Round about the cauldron go;

SECOND BEAR
>In the jug of water throw.

THREE BEARS
>Double, double toil and trouble;
>Fire burn and cauldron bubble.

FIRST BEAR
>Oats of Uncle Toby shake;
>In the cauldron boil and bake.

SECOND BEAR
>Dash of salt, and cup of milk.
>Stir and stir 'til smooth as silk.

THIRD BEAR
>Now to add a bit of honey;
>Making sure it's not too runny.

FIRST BEAR
>Chicken liver, ox's tail,
>And a giant juicy snail.

GOLDILOCKS runs from the stage with her hand over her mouth.

THREE BEARS
>Double, double toil and trouble;
>Fire burn and cauldron bubble.

KING ARTHUR
>Stop, stop, I pray you. This is not appropriate so soon after dinner.

JESTER shoos the THREE BEARS off stage, GOLDILOCKS returns wiping her mouth.

JESTER
>Sorry my Lord, maybe you would care for something else? Maybe… Hansel and Gretel?

KING ARTHUR
>Proceed.

JESTER claps his hands. Enter a bedraggled looking GRETEL.

GRETEL
>Hansel, Hansel, where for art thou Hansel?

GRETEL bursts into tears. All give HANSEL a disapproving look.

HANSEL
>I thought she vas following me.

KING ARTHUR
>I think it's best we see something else.

Exit GRETEL.

JESTER
>How about the tragedy of Ham-Let? I hear the narrator is excellent.

KING ARTHUR
>Very well then.

Enter 3 LITTLE PIGS.

JESTER *(as narrator)*
> Once upon a time three cute little pigs visited a village
> and their names were First Ham, Second Ham and Third
> Ham. The pigs where so cute and small that everybody in
> the village fell in love with them and asked them to stay.
> So, the pigs asked themselves a very important question.

3 LITTLE PIGS
> To let or not to let, that is the question.

JESTER *(as narrator)*
> And so, the first Ham let a house of straw.

FIRST HAM
> I let a house of straw.

JESTER (as narrator)
> The second Ham let a house of sticks.

SECOND HAM
> I let a house of sticks.

JESTER *(as narrator)*
> And the third Ham let a house of bricks.

THIRD HAM
> I let a house of bricks.

JESTER *(as narrator)*
> And they lived there happily, until one day along came a
> big bad wolf…

BIG BAD WOLF *(interrupts)*
> Ah - I have already seen this one! Perhaps another play?
> Something romantic for the ladies? Like… Cinderella?

GUINEVERE
>Oh, yes Arthur dear, please. Cinderella is my favourite.

Exit 3 LITTLE PIGS.

KING ARTHUR
>Jester, do we have such a play?

JESTER
>My lord I'm afraid we do, but the actors are of the lowest sort.

KING ARTHUR
>*(Reads the program)* "A tedious brief scene of young Prince Charming and Cinderella, a joyful tragedy".
>
>I do not recall the story of Cinderella being a tragedy?

JESTER
>I believe it is the alternative ending, my Lord.

GUINEVERE
>We will hear it.

JESTER
>No, my noble lady, it is not for you. I have heard it over, and it is nothing.

KING ARTHUR
>We will hear that play. Go bring them in and take your places, ladies.

JESTER
>As you wish, my lord. Here comes the prologue.

Enter 3 BLIND MICE as Prologue.

BLIND MICE 1
>If we offend, it is with our good will.

BLIND MICE 2
>That you should think, we come not to offend.

BLIND MICE 3
>But with good will.

BLIND MICE 1
>To show our simple skill.

BLIND MICE 2
>That is the true beginning from the end.

BLIND MICE 3
>The actors are at hand and by their show.

BLIND MICE 1
>You shall know all that you are like to know.

WICKED STEPMOTHER
>Why, it is the blind leading the blind.

GUINEVERE
>Are there three prologues or one?

KING ARTHUR
>Their speech was like a tangled chain. Not impaired but all disordered. Who is next?

BLIND MICE 1
>Ladies and gentlemen.

BLIND MICE 2
>Perchance you wonder at this show.

BLIND MICE 3
>But wonder on till truth makes all things plain.

BLIND MICE 1
>This man is Prince Charming.

Enter PUSS 'N BOOT (as Prince Charming) walks to front of stage and strikes a pose.

BLIND MICE 2
>This is ugly step sister one.

Enter PRINCE CHARMING (as Ugly Step Sister One) walks to front of stage and strikes a pose.

BLIND MICE 3
>And this is ugly step sister two.

Enter RAPUNZEL (as Ugly Step Sister Two) walks to front of stage and strikes a pose.

BLIND MICE 2
>And this beautiful lady is Cinderella.

Enter TROLL (as Cinderella) with a bucket (hidden in the bucket is a dress and a stiletto shoe) walks to front of stage and strikes a pose.

BLIND MICE 1
>She lives with her ugly step sisters, who force her to do all the household chores.

RAPUNZEL and PRINCE CHARMING (as ugly step sisters) order TROLL to scrub the floors.

BLIND MICE 2
>One day, the Prince decides to throw a ball. He invites all the maidens in the land, so he can select one to be his bride.

PUSS 'N BOOTS (as Prince Charming) gives an invitation to the ugly step sisters. Exit PUSS 'N BOOTS.

BLIND MICE 3
>As the two ugly step sisters leave for the ball, poor
>Cinderella weeps in despair for she is forbidden to go.

Exit RAPUNZEL and PRINCE CHARMING.

TROLL
>Oh boohoo, why won't they let me go to the ball?

TROLL sobs loudly.

BLIND MICE 2
>Then suddenly Cinderella's fairy god mother magically
>appears.

Enter RAPUNZEL (as Fairy Godmother).

BLIND MICE 1
>And turns her rags into a brand new super sparkly pretty
>dress.

*RAPUNZEL (as Fairy Godmother) waves her wand over the
bucket and TROLL draws out the dress hidden within it.*

BLIND MICE 2
>And a glass slipper.

*TROLL draws out of the bucket a single stiletto shoe. TROLL puts
the dress on over his costume. Enter STRAW MAN with a
wheelbarrow with a pumpkin in it. STRAW MAN lifts up the
pumpkin in the air above his head.*

BLIND MICE 3
>Taking a pumpkin, she turns it into a carriage.

*RAPUNZEL (as Fairy Godmother) taps the pumpkin with her
wand and STRAW MAN dramatically places it back into the
wheelbarrow. Exit STRAW MAN.*

BLIND MICE 1
> And a mouse into a horse.

RAPUNZEL (as Fairy Godmother) taps BLIND MICE 3 with her wand turning him into a horse. BLIND MICE 3 trots over to stand in front of the wheelbarrow.

BLIND MICE 2
> To take her to the ball.

TROLL (as Cinderella) starts to push the wheelbarrow off stage. RAPUNZEL (as Fairy Godmother) blocks TROLL from exiting.

BLIND MICE 1
> But, her fairy godmother warned her to be home before midnight.

BLIND MICE 2
> For at midnight the spell would be broken.

BLIND MICE 1
> And everything would change back to as it was.

BLIND MICE 2
> Cinderella promised she would return before midnight.

BLIND MICE 1
> And departed in her carriage.

Exit TROLL with the wheelbarrow, and BLIND MICE 3 (as a horse). Exit RAPUNZEL with the bucket.

BLIND MICE 1
> Now, fair audience we cordially invite you to join our actors at the ball.

Enter PRINCE CHARMING (as Ball) with a disco ball.

PRINCE CHARMING
> In this same interlude it doth befall,

That I, Prince Charming, present'th ball.
Not such a ball, as I would have you think,
But more a discotheque with lights that blink.
At which, the prince and servant girl did meet,
And there they boogied to my disco beat.

This ball, big wig and golden chain doth show,
That I am that same ball; it's my cameo.
Beneath this ball, held high and shining bright,
The two lovebirds will groove throughout the night.

GUINEVERE
Would you desire gold and hair to speak better?

GOLDILOCKS
It is the wittiest disco I have ever heard discourse.

BIG BAD WOLF
Why this event speaks for itself.

KING ARTHUR
Silence, Prince Charming draws near the ball.

PUSS 'N BOOTS
O grim looked night! O night with hue so black!
O night, whichever art, when day is not!
O night, O night! Alack, alack, alack.
No maiden fair, do I see, in this spot.
And thou, O ball, O sweet O lovely ball,
O play a tune to make this party rock,
Thou ball, O ball, O sweet and lovely ball
A song, to make, to me, the women flock!

Ball plays a tune.

Top tune ball! That ought to do it.

KING ARTHUR
The ball, I think, being sensible should play something
else.

PUSS 'N BOOTS

> No, in truth sir, he should not "that ought to do it" is
> Cinderella's cue. She is to enter now and I spy her across
> the room. You shall see, this will happen as I say. Yonder
> she comes.

TROLL

> O ball, from a distance have I heard thy bass.
> And long I have yearned to come to this place.
> To thy tunes, I always loved to bop,
> But alas my partner was my mop.

PUSS 'N BOOTS

> I see a voice! It is time to make my move,
> And show this fair lady, how the prince can groove.

TROLL

> The prince! Thou art my prince I think?

PUSS 'N BOOTS

> Think what thou wilt, for I am the Lord of Dance.
> And like Travolta, I do roll.

TROLL

> And I, like Olivia am your doll.

*They have a dance off, each performing a series of ridiculous
dance moves, challenging the other to come up with something
better.*

PUSS 'N BOOTS

> O, kiss me now my honeybee.

TROLL

> Oh no! Not here for all to see!

PUSS 'N BOOTS

> Wilt thou meet me outside yonder gate?

TROLL

> Sure thing, as long as I'm not late.

Exit PUSS 'N BOOT & TROLL in different directions.

PRINCE CHARMING

> Thus, have I, Ball, my part discharged so.
> And being done, thus Ball away doth go.

Exit PRINCE CHARMING.

WICKED STEPMOTHER

> This is the silliest stuff that ever I have heard.

KING ARTHUR

> Well if the ball has finished it must be nearly midnight.

GUINEVERE

> Here comes the Pumpkin.

Enter STRAW MAN with wheelbarrow and pumpkin. STRAW MAN picks up the pumpkin.

STRAW MAN

> You ladies – whose minds are slow of wit.
> I am here to tell you, this pumpkin, is not a pumpkin.
> But is a pumpkin that has been transformed into a
> carriage.

STRAW MAN places the pumpkin back into the wheelbarrow.

> And hence to pumpkin will it return at midnight's stroke.
> When this pumpkin, that it not a pumpkin, will be a
> pumpkin once again.

KING ARTHUR

> Well explained, good man.

GUINEVERE

> Did he just call us dumb?

HANSEL
>Look, here is the clock.

Enter RAPUNZEL (as Clock).

RAPUNZEL
>These hands do the current time present,
>Myself the town clock do seem to be.

BIG BAD WOLF
>A timely entrance clock.

HANSEL
>It appears her hands are all in a muddle.

RED RIDING HOOD
>Is that a quarter to or ten to midnight?

RAPUNZEL
>Look, all that I have to say, is, to tell you that these hands
>tell the time, I am the town clock, this is my face, and this
>is my bell.

KING ARTHUR
>Well said. Here comes Cinderella.

Enter TROLL (as Cinderella) holding a stiletto shoe.

TROLL
>This is the gate. Where is my love?

*RAPUNZEL (as Clock) rings bell 12 times. TROLL drops stiletto
shoe. STRAW MAN takes the pumpkin out of the wheelbarrow and
places it on the floor.*

TROLL
>It's Midnight!

*Exit TROLL, RAPUNZEL and STRAW MAN with the
wheelbarrow.*

RED RIDING HOOD
> Well, chimed clock.

WICKED STEPMOTHER
> Well run, Cinderella.

KING ARTHUR
> Excellent transformation pumpkin!

BIG BAD WOLF
> And then came Prince Charming.

Enter PUSS 'N BOOTS (as Prince Charming).

PUSS 'N BOOTS
> Sweet Moon, I thank thee for thy sunny beams;
> I thank thee, Moon, for shining now so bright;
> For, by thy gracious, golden, glittering gleams,
> I trust to take of truest maidens' sight.
> But stay, O spite!
> O curse this night,
> What dreadful sole is here!

PUSS 'N BOOTS (as Prince Charming) picks up the stiletto shoe.

> Eyes, do you see?
> How can it be?
> O dainty shoe! O dear!
> Thy slipper good,
> Where once you stood!
> O Fates, come, come.
> Cut thread and thrum,
> Quail, crush, conclude and quell.

HANSEL
> It's bit over the top.

RED RINDING HOOD
>It's not like she is dead.

PUSS 'N BOOTS *(holding up stiletto shoe)*
>She surely was the girl I rated,
>But alas she hath disintegrated.
>Come tear, confound,
>Out, sword, and wound.
>The pap of Charming.
>Ay, that left pap,
>Where heart doth hop,
>Thus die I, thus, thus, thus.

PUSS 'N Boots stabs himself dramatically with the heel of the stiletto shoe.

>Now am I dead,
>Now am I fled;
>My soul is in the sky:
>Tongue, lose thy light;
>Pumpkin take flight:
>Now die, die, die, die, die.

PUSS 'N BOOTS dies.

KING ARTHUR
>This is indeed a tragedy.

GUINEVERE
>Why look Cinderella returns.

Enter TROLL (as Cinderella).

TROLL
>When I last here withdrew,
>Methinks I lost my shoe.

Sees PUSS 'N BOOTS.

Asleep, my love?
What, dead, my dove?
O sweet Prince, arise!
Speak, speak. Quite dumb?
Dead? Dead! *(He cries)*

A tomb must cover thy sweet eyes.
These lily lips,
This cherry nose,
These yellow cowslip cheeks,
Are gone, are gone:
Lovers, make moan:
His eyes were green as leeks.
Tongue, not a word:
Come, trusty sword;
Come, blade, my breast imbrue:

TROLL stabs himself with heel of the stiletto shoe.

And, farewell, friends;
Thus Cinderella ends:
Adieu, adieu, adieu.

TROLL dies.

KING ARTHUR
Clock and Pumpkin are left to bury the dead.

JESTER
Yes, and Ball too.

PUSS 'N BOOTS *(sitting up)*
No, I assure you the ball finished at midnight and all have
departed. Will it please you to see the epilogue or perhaps
you would like to hear a dance?

KING ARTHUR
No epilogue, I pray you; for your play needs no excuse.
Never excuse; for when the players are all dead, there
need none to be blamed. Come, take your bow.

The actors bow and the guests applaud.

KING ARTHUR
> And now my bride, my love, let us dance.

They all dance. (Disco Music)

PETER & PAN clap their hands the music stops and all freeze.

PAN
> If we fellows have offended,

PETER
> Think but this, and all is mended,

PAN
> That you have but slumbered here,

PETER
> While these visions did appear.

PAN
> And this weak and idle theme,

PETER
> No more yielding but a dream.

PAN
> Give me your hands if we be friends,

PETER
> And Peter-

PAN
> And Pan-

PETER
> Shall restore amends.

They clap and the dance continues. The End.

Made in the USA
Middletown, DE
18 February 2020